The Sesame Street Storybook Alphabet

Featuring Jim Henson's Sesame Street Muppets

by Linda Hayward

Illustrated by Tom Cooke

A SESAME STREET/GOLDEN PRESS BOOK
Published by Western Publishing Company, Inc.
in conjunction with Children's Television Workshop

Chicken Little

Goldilocks and the Three Bears

The Ugly Duckling

The Three Billy Goats Gruff

Old King Cole

Mary Had a Little Lamb

The Princess and the Pea

Oven

The Gingerbread Man

The Three Little Pigs

Snow White and the Seven Dwarfs

S

Star

Twinkle, twinkle, little star. Let me count how many there are.

Twinkle, Twinkle, Little Star

Rapunzel

Rain, Rain, Go Away

W

Wand

The Princess Who Never Laughed